Afterlight

Afterlight

Marc Hudson   The University of Massachusetts Press

Copyright © 1983 by
The University of Massachusetts Press
All rights reserved
Printed in the United States of America
Library of Congress Cataloging in Publication Data
Hudson, Marc, 1947–
Afterlight.
I. Title.
PS3558.U3114A69   1983   811'.54   83–10441
ISBN 0–87023–413–7
ISBN 0–87023–414–5 (pbk.)

*For George Afton Hudson
and Edith Goldsmith Hudson*

Contents

1

For Wang Wei

To say water and the waterbirds,
fog that drifts in spindles from the north,
an intelligence not quite articulate,
the gull hastening and beyond him the white hover,
the crested wing of the Olympic Range,
I need to learn the character for silence.
I listen across twelve centuries to your music,

see the oxen on the wide green terrace,
a knot of men struggling with a wagon
and the one in all that scene who isn't working.

Reading Chretien by Hood Canal

for David Fowler

1

Silence all afternoon.
Then a few kinglets,
sparks blown
through dark timber.

Now the last rigs
loaded with fir
trundle down from the clearcuts.

A glass of water
on my desk
shines by Chretien's book.

The Canal is at ebb—
a smell of harvest,
drying windrows of kelp,
dead crustaceans.

Chretien sat late
but left unfinished
the *Conte del Graal*
which I turn to at twilight.

As I read
dark scribes
move over the stiffened parchment
of the tideland.

2

Years ago, the boy set out,
crossed the footbridge
where the stream paused
for a pool of blue iris.

In an oval window
the mother sat weaving
a blindfold journey

for her son—
thin white trees like birch
by a road or a river.

He heard the ringing of branches
against breastplates,
and mistook armed men for angels.

In his heart an image stayed
of a high stone-ringed pool,
a girl half-quarried from light.

Call that journey loss
and the boy its pilgrim.
He must travel where wind
has made the plain enormous,

where cart tracks appear
and disappear
in the blowing grass,
and funeral fires
smoulder on the headlands.

Over dust and scoria,
the map of hunger
with its legend of gray
bread, he travels.

3

At nightfall,
an old man drifts on the water,
a few graylings in his creel.

The boy calls from the shore,
asks about shelter.

Where the alder is thick,
where the river turns and slows,
he is told,
the fisherking receives
all strangers.

Later, he is seated by the fire,
the glowing andirons
in the shape of greyhounds.

The lame king lies on his side,
half-listening,
half-withheld,
like a dying root-bare tree.

Then a cup is borne in
of gold and niello
worked with such care
each incision
of rose or torso
is like a moon or a sun.

The dark-eyed servant
paces the floor;
another follows
with a spear of gray ash.
Blood falls
on the hot flags.

The boy asks nothing
of these marvels.
Three times they pass
and three times he sees them
and is silent.

After the luminous
entertainments,
after swan and almond milk,
and the red wine,
he drowses by the fire.

4

I've heard the sea
tell a similar legend,
all night in his insomnia
pacing the tideland,

and gone out
into the still world
between two breakers.

Chretien, all is made
and unmade
in the moonlight.

The Saxons
called waves fallow:
they are like fields in winter,
eroded furrows
where lost things gleam.

On such nights
I have prayed
and learned this much—
my two hands,
the barnacle and its stone,
are brother orphans.

5

Chretien, your book
and the tideland
reeking of salt and iodine,
the margin of sea-marked carrion.

Chretien, your book
and the history of iron,
men soldering the metal shrouds
for their sleeping daughters.

We kneel on this earth
as before an open grave.

6

Each day it passes before us,
the Cup with its deep incisions of Love itself,
Grail of the sea-worn clear-cut ridges
and the coppery bracelets of chiton,
of light only at home in eyeholes of dust,
intaglio of spirit grooved deep in rock and flesh,

Cup with a seed of blood planted in its chest.

Night, and the Dipper is nearly overhead.

Brush fires gutter on the windy ridges;
and in the curved harbors across the Canal—
docklights, swinging lamps of gillnetters.

I kindle a small fire of alder and driftwood,
listen to the wrenbone twigs as they catch.
When I close my eyes, the garden's there—
a poise of light in petal and leaf,
buds nudging into flame, even the thorn
singing—

these moments at the verge of sleep,
a sinking fire, Chretien,
water and moonlight
loosely rooted
in the furrows.

Dewato

The crows of Dewato
live in a ruined house.
I went there once
in a thin snow

though I saw very little
it stayed with me
like a grief
not well understood

but gone back to—
the shack there of cinderblocks
on the gravel bank,
the absent look of the water

the way it said nothing
that gray afternoon
and I seemed to glance
over the bones of the estuary

at a barren tree
with the mummies of children
sewn into its leaves.
I looked again

and a slow hand
moved back into the waves:
only a broken alder
shading the drained mud.

Home

Here is my home. Here heap my cairn
at just this hour some morning.
The silence of my corpse
will not be terrifying—
the kinglets with their yellow crests
will cross before the sun
and their cries will be pleasant to hear.

In each of us there is a country—
I have known a man at home in the tundra,
a seeker of barrows and old flints;
and another, a woman,
in the windy grasses of an island.

But here I would have you
heap my cairn, this slippery cleft
of sword ferns, knobs
of young Boletus
and the sound of freshets
curving cedarwood—
the undercolor of my blood
as I close my eyes
like pebbles in that stream.

Late Winter Sky

Dark masses of trees blowing & stars,
shorelights, Orion
setting over the Olympics,
Cassiopeia like a gaunt wing—

surely these are beings,
perhaps those women of Sumer
who calmly took the poison
& put on their fillets of gold & silver
as they lay down
or dolphins flanked with suns
leaping out for an instant—

I see them from my setting planet,
the winter star
that even now is shuddering
in a blind green light.

Afterlight

Ringing over the water in the afterlight—
wingbeats of scoters.
Grebe take on the quiet of words
on earthen walls,
a dark script carefully rendered.
And soon a stillness of wings,
the white hover of that mountain range
will say your distance, orphan,
the moon like the flat of a hand
against your brow.

You will go from thing to thing
like a child in his last illness
looking straight at his mother and frowning.

Elegy for Martin Heidegger

Think of stones in the tideland now half sunk in gravel,
clouds and cloud islands flattening in the afterlight.
Think of a man's duration, oyster middens at the rivermouth,
layer on layer of covered dishes, caskets elaborately carved
with reticent animals, remains no more than silt
tracked by the turnstone.

And the child Earth sleeps on,
sleeps in the raying flesh of the ascidian,
in the watery chains of red algae, the raw delicate trees
washed ashore. The sea rises and falls in her locket.
It is a breathing mirror whose every image
is the child asleep, the gray-haired dreamer
whose first word is still forming.

The house in the wind shadow of the mountain,
the low-eaved house that sheltered the passers-by
as they sat at cards or slept on the heavy benches,
the high straight beam like the keelson of a ship,
cradle and coffin tree and the icon in its corner,
are abandoned, as a child leaves its things in the rain
when called home: Martin Heidegger is dead.
A greater stillness than thought has taken him.
Think of clouds and cloud islands
over the one-horned mountain, the voyager steering
toward that bronze door and the hearth beyond.

Hawk

for Ariah

In your dream the hawk was soaring
over the uprush of red cedar, the hurried plunge of fir,
over shocks of water crashing from the glacier's
claw. Sparrows wheeled fearfully calling over the river
stunned with light. The hawk saw all:
filaments of moss on the red talus,
ferns curving in the spore-blown sun, an ant emerging
with a larva in his pincers, swarms of clouded sulfurs,
the gritty river itself grinding and twisting through boulders.
So much she'd seen and possessed:
lakes dancing like stones, ridges ordered
beneath her talons. But now the blinds of light were flung aside,
the sun was roaring, enormous, the hawk could dive into that
    eye.
The world below at its brightest moment
was a shadow to this, the dream
no dream but the zone where a sleeping woman ·
reaches into the hawk and seizes daybreak.

A Road in the Willapa Hills

for Helen

Among roads deadending in clearcuts,
rotting trestles of cedar,
among streams forced
into culverts, and poisoned
alder, we came on a road
leading elsewhere. It didn't swerve
north to KO Peak and the transmitters,
nor into fresh-cut slopes
where the living blaze still whirls
in stumps of fir.
It was a road unnumbered
by Weyerhauser, a trace
with more twig ends than Gray's River
or our veins. We had no map
but the one we held between us,
incomplete as yet, half-penciled in,
yet we were certain it would lead us
deep into the Willapas, over Gray's
Divide, the rivers and ridges
healing around us
with a force equal to our lives.

Climbing Together

When, after love,
a man pulls gently from a woman
and they lie together
barely touching,
their eyes move far over slopes
and memories of slopes, difficult grips
in stone, the floating bodies they were
almost without faces,
the bitter landscape with only a naked buzzing
and hatred like chalk
and the moment after when they swung
beyond whatever rope held them to their bones
and time that had been so empty,
or else a wound,
enclosed and completed them—
for one heartbeat
the blood winds on a strange path
carrying oxygen
to everything that breathes
and to the plumes
of the yet unborn.

Above Moraine Park

You were playing the recorder
on a ridge of drift and till,
some old French round,
light bird notes
at the timberline.

I'd just identified a lavender
flower I hadn't known—
Davidson's penstemon—,

and you had found
this song to practice
near a lip of snow
overhanging
the clearest water.

Helen, I could not name you then—
for centuries in summer
penstemon and water,
and now this song
which hadn't been there before.

At Suthurstrond

Being at the sea wall, you have to talk loud
or not all.
The ocean plays havoc with syntax, makes off
with whole clauses
giving a sudden random emphasis
when none was meant.
Yet masses of waves breaking on a rocky headland
are not unlike in rhythm
the looser periods of Pound and Homer,
blocks of prose
in newspaper even, whatever cadence speech takes on
when not faking
or trying out the trumpery of some Alcaic—
a natural iambus
the sea's foot and the tireless wagging human tongue.
I know this
a long and tedious introduction
but say the North Atlantic
breaking on Suthurstrond is my instructor.
I've listened
until my ears are chafed and burning
as the waves
wildly working under seven crosswinds
and a steady sun.
A cormorant just now went by like a crossbow,
heart or sea
skipped a beat, I saw you stepping on the slick
rime sheath
of tideland rocks and all the white cobble
a wave becomes
as land tries also to advance on the verge
and limit
it can't overstep, as we all do, our lines
breaking as they
must in random disarray as we speak
what, breathless,
we always meant to, as Homer did of Helen
the one beloved.

At Berkeley Park

This moment is the only window.
Here on its sill, there are waterfalls, glaciers, streams
in the rough stone vases
they've cut for themselves.

Nearer the heart of the room—
a hawk-mitred pine, a gray basin wall
with its fault lines, its lines of snowmelt
like long-legged shorebirds.

Nearer still—
a field of yellow anthered
avalanche lilies
where a god is saying

Thus do I appear.

Island

for Gala FitzGerald

I

I know this island.
A wind from this moment blows the light off the sea,
the far crests flinted with silver.
A seal eases from its ledge in the wavesmoke.
Bushes and stones stir and brighten.
A kingfisher hangs in the air, rapidly beating its wings.
It was here the dream began.

I hear the old voices,
the island loud in the stones and rattling nighthawk,
the silence of the yellowing brome
before the wind picks up toward evening,
tethered seeds like small boats along a pier.
The surf makes a rush and whorl round each feather
of the goose barnacles.
Sieved plankton whistle thinly as they die.

The woman who came from the gray rock
goes before me in the dream.
Call her bridgemaker, weaver of the far wave:
in her name is the promise of return.
But I must go it alone like the hemlock
pulled over in the last storm and tilting into the surf,
barnacles and pennants of moss on the raw limbs.

Waiting to cross, each runnel appears
deeper than hell, each trough holds a thousand coffins.
I see a pod of killer whales out on the Sound.
The small boatmen are in danger of swamping.
If the waves say anything, it is
Go now. Leave your shell
as foothold for the young.

2

I had no skin
only bones and the veins draping them
like fishnet on a gunwale.

I stood in the mantle of a wave,
waiting for my body,
shivering.

Strangers came, seal faces,
ravens overhead complaining,
crabs with their swiveling eyestalks.

Fear makes a bad meal,
I heard one say,
Let the sea cure him.

So they left me there
like driftwood
or fog on the headland.

3

I fell asleep in the gray moss of the waves,
the great moonweeds swaying and toppling.
It seems I entered a shell or the turreted silence
of the ocean. It's hard to recall—
the moon was young then and closer,
I could discern its work in the ribs of diatoms and the hardening
chalk.
I slept a long time in the drift of those skeletons.

4

Far on the rocks in the fog
the gulls were crying.
Over the steady wavechant
I heard voices and oarstrokes,
men calling the blooded kokanee.

That night I joined them
in the aldersmoke and starlight.
I stood in a circle without fear
listening to flutebone and rattle
as animals walked from the fire.

Beyond the glinting sealrock,
I saw children and salmon
on a ladder of moons.
Song was to help them
from crescent to crescent,
so I raised my voice with the others.

From then on, sleep was broken.
I tumbled in the wrack
without a body of my own.

5

He came again, the one who'd spoken,
he tended the waves
as if they were a furnace,
sunkiln he called them.

*These are the only masks
worth having*, he said,
*these wet guts, these fishbones.
Knowledge is breath and change.
You may never leave the wave
so make your body of its breaking.*

6

Though you fall away in the dark,
fall without hindrance
from ledge to ledge, the moon making
short work of whatever distinction
your face had,
though you fall with the faceless bodies,
the crescent scars of your own nails
on the thighs of the victims,
though your maggot vanishes and you never find it
on earth again,
say to the tall grass, the delicate seedchains:
    I go looking
to the lichen-spotted groundling nighthawk:
    I go looking
to the deadly angels, the veiled amanitas:
    I go looking

to the crests and blazons of all lifechains:
  I go looking

7

A shearwater dives, sheathing itself in light.
The wave rides forward out of the sun
and, with it, all I will ever love—
the hemlock where the heron perches, a shred of fog
that loosens and moves slowly off,
the light changing from green to pewter, changing constantly
as the elements respect no division,
the purple crabs scrambling through the sedge in great numbers,
decisively as under one command,
the seal, the woman, the pivoting surge of the sea itself,
that moon-leashed leviathan,
and the tall, crowned grasses striding toward death.
With these I lean toward what I know
and will come to know as I listen
to the voices of the island:

Pulse after pulse
the sun drives the bloodscrews, the wedges of beginning
into each crack of time.
The seal laughs in the wave,
the sickle moon cuts and cuts again
these cliffs. Nothing stays.
Not grass, not water, not even the sun.
Praise and pass on.

3

Painter at Dusk

At this hour he would listen
to the blind singer
under his window
and, beyond, the river approaching
through the willows.

He would leave his studio then
as if someone in the street
had called him out, called him
using an old nickname
he couldn't ignore.

It was twilight
and the mountains folded
like the robes of a sitting cardinal.
Some children were playing tag
and, as he passed, one of them
stopped and would remember.

Crossing the scythed field,
the ruts filling with leaves,
he could feel the dream coming on,
the stooks and the olive trees
soft as rainbeaten stone.

He had studied this hour—
the moon floating through blue
marble, the vineyards, the river
where he'd seen his death fully unsheathed
like a bird flying into a mirror.

Sixteenth-Century Icelandic Chair

Benedikt Narfasson made me,
carved runes on my back,
saying I belongd to Thorunn
Jonsdottir. Underneath
he cut a zodiac, ram and bull
and scales, as if to say
this is a chair for contemplation
of such things. After they beheaded
the Bishop of Holar, her father,
she kept much alone in my company.
She set me by a window
where her custom was to study
the changing light on the bay.
In fair weather, with a brisk wind
ships would drive beyond
the headland, soon lost in blowing
cloud. "Dragon-headed chair,"
she addressed me in a whisper,
"You too seem voyage-eager,
meant to glide under wind
after the keen-eyed one.
You too were branded by runes
and the knife made you beautiful.
The Bishop's daughter, and her chair,
peaceful as they seem, know this—
only in blood acts is knowledge born.
What Njal saw through burning timbers
by bloodtorch on the swarthy air—
each glacier cut bay and headland,
and the small men huddled there
watching fire gouge and scar
the hawk carving on his door, his eye
deep in its orbit—is what I see
sitting quietly here with my needles."

Dusting the Sill

Bend close to these mold-split husks,
beetles crimped as toenails.
Their bodies' one extravagance is a poor joke:
antennae twisted like handlebar moustaches.
Imagine the constriction of their lives—
to crawl the sill in a feeble routine of hunger
and pick your way through lint and spider shit,
to have in death the cheap endurance of a plastic charm,
the not quite smirking silence of an acquitted felon.

Goya saw them, the beetles clambering on the sill,
the sucked bodies where the spider hunched,
and heard the carts trundling by the Prado
and the Puerta del Sol. His housekeeper was cleaning
by the window, the small bodies and the lint
made a fragile bracelet. He saw the French reload and fire
straight into the clenched faces.
He'd sketched it on the wall with the gutter
for his palette; the mud caked very quickly.
That night he had the hated dream: God
had dragged Himself from the cave
and was swaying over the ditch, His beak
like a sparrow's feeding on berries.

Hanging at Galgahraun

The view from Gallow's Lava
lacks perspective,
the next headland is lost
in gull-loud fog.
I can't think
it will ever clear.
I must be satisfied
with this poor sketch—
gray gannets
on the lava tongues, and these gray
tarns skinned over with ice.
The sea's not worth
penciling in—
a leaden wash
of monotones.

I, Egil Magnusson,
take leave of wife, daughter,
my one hectare of frost-
bitten turnips, and this
whey-faced confessor
bland as a butterknife.
I like the thin-lipped
hangman better.
His parish
is well provided for.

Good-bye Spinoza,
Good-bye St. Augustine—
this is man, this finite extension
in a tight noose.
Good-bye Theseus and Sophocles—
this is the winding
blood-dark labyrinth
robed in seven coils
of imported hemp.
And good luck my soul,
may you leak
through the gratings of my ribs,
lonely vapor to the last.

And you, body,
in your hand-me-down
motley of the elements,
guest of honor
at the raven's banquet,
farewell! Make this
impoverished soil
somewhat less sour.

George Vancouver's Death Dream

At Petersham   May 1798

Only the elms, thank God, the loud elms.
I was dreaming, John, a melancholy dream.
A cold sea broke on columns of basalt.
Rain fell; stopped; came on harder, and then was
Still. Waves worked less and less. I heard the small
Streams hurry down with their stony voices.
It was a quiet desolation—
Cobble like scoria, firebroken rock
And a strange kelp with bloody ragged warts
Of blossom. That was all, those streams in spate
Falling away, bits of shell underfoot.

I saw ahead of me a crescent beach
Of milk-white barren sand. Two sharp-adzed poles
Were planted there with heads on them. Great, great
Had been the wrath that skewered them, those scalps
Punched through and folded back like rag. I cried,
"Cook! Poor Cook! What have they done?" (I
Could not mistake that severe brow, those thin
Lips bitten and pulled from the teeth in pain—
Like salt in the slab of his butchered back
His fate's in me.) The other, John, was mine.

I must have shouted loud for you to hear
Over the elms. You were kind to stir
From your little sleep; faithful you have been
Scribbling these journals and tending your sick
Brother: it shows in your face, sallow, drawn,
Not like it was a year ago, though mine
Is sunken more, the skull here and here
Breaks nearly through the skin, doesn't it?
A hard seed splitting through its husk—so men
Carry their death, and lie at last in the
Grave. You know my will; I've thought on this long
Days by the window: a plain common grave
I want, no costly marble, and these words
As epitaph: Captain George Vancouver Died
In The Year 1798.

Neither the day of my death, nor that I
Was an officer in the King's Navy.
I would be forgot. . . .
                    But damn Thomas Pitt,
Damn his eyes, for caneing me. Proud bastard,
I knew from my first look at him he'd be
Trouble: those damned insolent eyes. And so
He was. Foul-mouthing me behind my back,
Sketching caricatures. I caught him at it,
Flogged 'im; he spat; I kept him in the bilboes
'Til his legs broke out in sores; discharged him
In Owyhee. I honestly hoped he'd
Die—but he comes back Baron Camelford
And a bloody vengeance on his mind.
No wonder I dream of Cook and his hard
Death. All who took that voyage are tainted
With violence. At the lava's edge, they
Held him under and finished him with clubs
And iron knives, they who'd worshipped him,
Crying, "Erono! Erono!" when he
First came ashore, feasted on his flesh.
And now this horrid riot in which Europe
Is thrown, wave after wave of smoking blood—
We wake into nightmare, the loud elms, John,
What do they mean?
                    So, so, I'll quieten.
It was thinking on Camelford. . . . I'm sure
He paid Gillray for the cartoon, and thus
Had his revenge. I'm made the laughingstock
Of London now. "Kamehameha's Cloak,"
They whisper slyly, "have you given it
Yet to King George?" At times, I must admit,
None of it matters—I turn to the wall
And dream; recall my dream's beginning.

Memory gives back a day six years gone.
It was then first light, the thirtieth of April.
Utter silence but for the creak of ropes,
Far faint cries of white-headed eagles.
Southward mountains stood free of cloud, their sheer

Basalt streaming with freshets. Fir pollen
Drifted from onshore. Our topgallants set,
The wind bore us into the dawn: was this
The Passage—that low haze eastward like grain
And poppies? According to Purchas,
De Fuca sailed for twenty days past headlands
Deep in blossom, dark loam; and reached the Atlantic.
Light came stronger and the wind increased.
I grasped a shroud to stay my wonder.
It all comes back—the blue glare of glaciers,
Foam flakes, gulls driven like spume from a wave,
The wrinkled sea, like a torch, lit from within.
The brilliance floods back. I knew as a god
The tidal bore of rivers, the blue pulse
Of this planet; for an instant I knew
All of it lives, lives not one jot less than
This hand you clench. . . .
                              There is no Passage:
De Fuca, if he lived at all, a drunk
Liar, likewise Meares, and Dalrymple—
For good reason we sailed on April First.
No Passage there, though wealth enough in furs;
Fair trade they'll get, those Nootka savages—
For skins and fish, smallpox and slavery;
Copper for their great cedars. . . .
                              I am sick
At what I've seen, the hard, hard usages
And the earth is so fair. . . .
                              Go to bed now,
A gray light strengthens through the copse beyond,
The elms subside. They say men die most at dawn.
But today I'll hear milk carts passing,
Haloos of bargemen from the Thames. Today,
At least, and a few days more, I'll listen
To the river drifting toward London,
Mothers calling at nightfall from doorsteps.
Would you open the curtains before you go—
There, St. Peter's spire, like a mast it is.
In all my travels I never clapped eyes
On a more beautiful spot than this.
Here would I live and here I would die.

36

A German Printmaker

The long nights were good for work.
His elbows outspread on the plank table,
the unshuttered kerosene lamp
beside the block of ash
his burin was poised over,
he would wait until the image
had crookt his fingers
like stunted hornbeam,
like kneeling pensioners,
then he would lean his full weight
into the blade.

What is man
but a deep chisel stroke
in a difficult wood?
Barlach and Kollwitz had taught him—
best to work in ash.
Accepting his limits
he needed ever less,
pride and defiance maybe
like a miner when he goes down the pit
nothing round him
but coal and stone and iron.

Still, he had loved the softer woods.
The *Biblia Pauperum* was cut in pearwood;
sometimes he saw
folds of Gothic drapery
in the layers of its grain.

But walnut was his favorite.
The fragrance it gave off
submitting so easily to his blade
felt like forgiveness.
Cutting the sweet wood
he'd think of death
leaning over a cradle,
the mother interposed
between the child
and the dreaming knife,

and war
that snatched up walnut
for gunstocks.

So he turned again to conifer wood
from the Schwarzwald
and the iron-hard ash.
He thought of Paul Klee—
"I've had this war so long within . . .
it is only in memory
I dwell in the shattered world. . . ."
And Franz Marc trudging toward Verdun
in a dream of animals.

It was as they say—
the hard wood forced him to be simple,
drab as grief.
Yet he could raise a sweetness
out of the ash,
a mortal clinging odor
as of green pear and applewood.

It was any winter.
Through the whorls of ash
he could see them all—
gated towns like cairns
along a mountain waste
where men have passed;
the plains of Lutzen that bitter dawn,
rags of an icy fog
over the earthworks and shrouded cannon;
and the fires of Dresden
like marigolds in the frost
dying back to the seed;

All this resolved into a face,
a net of shadows and crowsfeet,
brutal and innocent
like the sheepshead gall of an oak;
or a child staring through a crumbled wall
at the steep white orchard and the one star.

Summer, Aeneas Valley

It is hard to face these hills
and not feel the thirst of being
in a dry land. Crumbling rock
like loaves too long in the sun,
yarrow easily bundled into a rushlight,
and lichen—green-gold beards of it
minutely branching on the deadfall,
dark, forking Cladonia on the bald summits—
these petrify
like the husks old stars give off.

Life is water
and the San Poil now
is but three steps across;
three steps more of aspen and alder
you face these baked hills,
the thick-barked ponderosas,
sparse, white-yellow grass
that already seems half flame.
Here a tree, a barred owl,
or a man without water
in a few days belong to the same species
of dust, adobe, and straw.

Late Garden

Here is September's garden,
this high meadow of stout-ribbed hellebore,
turrets of the poppy falling to earth.
The sun in his brightest helmet
is pale as Hector
stalked by vengeance.

The life of vision ends here.
No man can see beyond the lupine
unless he folds his sky
like blue linen,
scythes the grasses and marigolds
and lays them to rest
with the bones of the sun.

Winter, Aeneas Valley

The five parapets of Horn Hill
are dusted with snow; by the river
yellow doors in full sunlight
break from their hinges, the eyelids
of the aspen struck clean off.
Maybe the ledges of schist,
maybe they with their bundles of lichen,
their silvery weeds like brittle stars,
are as disinterested as they seem,
but the valley is thinning out.
At night the goat path
swings up the tableland toward Capella.
A manlike figure
shades his eyes and then steps out
the way the moon does early on,
not sure yet of its footing.
Because of the legends of wheat,
bread for the asking in the winter sky,
life always wants this elsewhere
and breaks free when it can.
As for us who remain,
we can pick the black moss from the branches
for our cakes and, under the broken ridge,
admire the talus of leaf-shaped stones
no more and no less than the poverty
rightfully ours in the end.

Okanogan Sleep

for Jody Wyatt

At dusk, Horn Hill
turns ruddy as a torch,
nighthawks swing out over the San Poil
and, when they dive,
that bass thrumming note is like a door
opening in the wind.
I have heard it before, often.

Night, and the moon is spinning
from its substance
a thin cloud
like the mantle of an ammonite.
Blue-white Vega burns near the zenith;
that high ancient meadow
mirrors this one—
bugloss, mullein, the red-orange of Arcturus
like a berry of Viburnum.
In this sparse land
sky is the greatest plenitude.

In certain of my dreams
the animals remove their masks
and are human;
the yellow pine, the fir
show their rings,
even sky is simply a man
of great reserve.

So sleep is a kind of walking
that takes me far
into the tamarack of Dugout Mountain,
the cool, glacial stands there
flaring more brightly as winter comes on.

Red Cedar

It comes back to me now, the dream I had of a great cedar,
its root staves tall as my shoulder; there was a door,
a slab of dark, heavy-scented mold, all around me a dust of
    water,
the sun in many spokes whirling.
Through the door were forms the tree held shining like larvae—
infants swaddled in shredded bark, naked long-eared mice
never to be weaned, skulls & femurs shingled with moss,
the likeness of a cadaver stitched with human hair,
eyes sealed with opercula—whole generations cloaked in cedar
journeying under the tree.

I think of a thin cloud near dusk, beyond the cloud
a ridge, a single tree at its summit barring the disc
of the sun, how its shadow was thrown toward me
into the cloud, a tree all of quartz in those curving folds,
rose quartz roped with light, issuing like blood from a portal—
so this tree tapers & flames, & the shore rekindles now,
the life of a people in its ruddy limbs.

Voices Overheard on a Night
of the Perseid Shower

Our being here was brief.
We too lay in the burnt grass
and counted those stars
like wind-borne thistle seed;

of a dusty afternoon,
gathered mussels from the San Poil—
where the aspen shadow was deepest
there we found them
like the beaks of nestlings;

and marveled at the caddis fly,
that strange donkey
hauling its cairn
under the stream.

Yarrow, pearly everlasting
become like straw this time of year,
and the mullein, with its torch bearing seed,
its great tongues of goat wool,
dies back to a whorl of earth.

Better than you we understood
hardness under the grasses,
the long, long aprons of talus.

Rock flakes because of iron,
like blood drying into crusts
resembling lichen—

those plants have no memory
and must loosen the memory
even from stones
where seed or blood has fallen.

A Natural History of the Fourteenth Century

1346

Four thousand French are dead at Crecy.
Crows sweep Edward's threshing floor,
random swaths
of the longbow's harvest.
A gardyn saw I ful of blosmy bowes . . .
On every bow the foules herde I synge. . . .
The boy who read
Guillaume de Lorris,
the carter from Bruges,
and blind King John
in his cloak of ermine,
his crest of peacock feathers,
lie side by side in the leveling rain.
Therewith a wind, unnethe it myghte be lesse,
Made in the leves grene a noyse softe. . . .

In the high meadow
by the moraine
lupine succeed avalanche
lilies. Blue keels of blossom
break on pumice soil.

1350

A ship founders on a ledge near Bergen,
its cargo wool and buboes,
ten thousand gross of the seeds of black peas,
pustules at groin and armpit.

Matrons in blue kerchiefs,
fishermen waiting for the weather to break,
have gathered on the beach.
The keel groans. Buoylike,
the minster bell is tolling.

Everywhere, the sulfur
stench of kelp and sea ooze.

Everywhere,
the circumference of the tolling bell
sweeping out from Bergen.

Petrels, with small worried cries,
skim the whitecaps. Cormorants
on the channel rocks
gaze toward Apocalypse.

The last harebell above the glacier
is *Campanula rotundifolia.*
Its blue is more fugitive than lupine,
it can lose the eye at dusk.

1355

Barna has finished his fresco.
The scaffolding is gone
from the nave of San Gimignano.

He studies his Passion
for the first time—
in an enclave of helmets,
the victim in his halter,
the soldier with tenpenny
nails and claw
hammer. These are well enough
done. Better is the frenzied
stupor of the crowd—
in the whites of their eyes
a cattlelike myopia.

He recalls the falconer
who carried a shrike in a cage.
Long after the falcon was lost
it turned and gleamed
in the shrike's fearful stare.

1379

Beards of rye are festering
with St. Anthony's fire.
God is near in the dark mycelia.

Before he dies
the foolish ploughboy
has visions sharp as a flagellant's,
can see in the crowns of spear thistles
hawkblaze of the Pentecost.

Arnica alpina—
its solitary stem
bears a single
yellow head
of nine strongly notched
ray florets.

Somewhere in this century
a man has fallen asleep.

Points of mica gleam
in recently cut
blocks of sandstone.

Swallows
with a sipping motion
take green-winged
ephemerae of the pond.

He walks in the visio of grief.
That sky is the deep
indigo of Jean de Berry's
Book of Hours.

In that grass,
the brilliant miniatures,
common things
memory has kept—
a daughter's comb,
a spindle whorl,
the path where she
turned, breaking
a sprig of rosemary.

They are bathed in absence
like the blueness of campanula
and have no possible use.

A man remembering
kneels in time
outside this time.
For him
all centuries are cloudshadow,
rock tumbled against rock
in fields of talus.

He hears the ballad
wind takes up once more—
all shall belong
to the province of memory.

Yet lupine, for a time,
was another sky
under the blinding glacier.

Last Rites

Grasses are blowing, russet plantain, tall jointed brome,
a swallow works in the wind like a farmer at harvest time.
It will be soon the fields are threshed and winnowed,
smoking like meal in a sieve.

It will be soon the soil grows thin
about the bonehouse and the stronghold of breath
gives in. What will we say
when hill and plough and fir tree,
words we thought would bear a steady yield,
are like alder poisoned, a common greenness suddenly
gone? Take these raw eroded hills,
the summit of KO Peak too steep to be logged
yet logged nonetheless. The cable slides
in the buzzard hook, the skinned tree skids down.
Our speech must have gone bad for this to happen.

The medievals knew the signs of death—
sharp nose, sunken eye, skin hard and parched
across the cheek. The priest would knock
at the sad door. He would housel that dust.

Earth sluiced away, scar after scar
on the Willapa Ridges, acrid smoulder
of the mill at Wauna, the silted rivermouth:
these are signs a man can read.

But how will he confess whose language fails him?

Soley

for Orn and Thordis

Grass does not grow in this wind—
only *Dryas octopetala,* "island of the sun,"
namesake of an ice age.
It blows in drifts over drumlins,
glacial landforms calling to mind
turf-covered burial mounds
where gold may lie, though the north wind
is robbing the farmer blind.

All the gold he has is in this flower
which grew under dirt-beaked glaciers
near acid bogs, and still haunts
cold places where only the wind
makes a killing. He jokes to his woman—
"Maybe there's money in soley."
"And gold in the wind," she answers,

considering it must hoard somewhere
so many lost harvests.
Tomorrow perhaps, or the day after,
the wind will slacken, and their daughter
will sit in the dooryard grass
plaiting soley into a necklace.

5

Some Gnomic Verses

Men will gouge elements from the earth,
Glacier scour gray stone,
Silt fatten the rivermouth.
Whimbrel and brant will fly in autumn,
Voices under Orion, salmon leap
In the hungry sun, the dying man
Unravel his maze. Love is hardest,
Hail coldest, glede burns
The child's hand. Sea will shuttle
Among islands, wind work
Mutable cloud, memory is endless.
Blue whale will breach gouted with blood,
Dolphin thrash in the purse seine,
Birds, at last light, sing.
Tears will scald the guilty sleeper,
The revenant come for his red meal,
Love is sweetest and most bitter.
Soft wood, apple and yew,
Is best to carve, copper to engrave,
Tungsten for the thin white flame.
First leaf is most sheer, coltsfoot
Earliest to flower, siskin lightest
Of birds. Time is cruelest
To creatures who remember. Man is the calendar
Kept by dust.

Walking to Dewato

The Trident Submarine Base is located on Hood Canal
near Bangor, Washington. Each Trident sub carries ten missiles,
each missile with at least ten nuclear warheads—
a force per sub equal to over a thousand Hiroshimas.

They called me to the door that evening,
    gulls on the beach below
crying out like children, unhappy
    to leave their play.

I saw no predator but beauty—
    grebe fishing the gold
as gleaners will bend to a furrow
    intent on gathering.

Sky there was island after island
    of steady harvest. And I
listened to the angelus of the scoters,
    wingbeats, mountains

and the deepening passage over them—
    to the north, Perseus,
and, low in the south, the Ploughman
    climbing the blue fields.

This was given then as the two crows
    will sometimes drop you
pebbles or as a stone will find
    itself in your hand,

an emblem of some danger:
    I thought then of Dewato,
white trees at a rivermouth, piers
    foundering in mud.

I thought of the crows I'd seen there,
    how they scratched a living
from the shore, cracking barnacles,
    scraping the tide of its flesh.

They rose at my coming with bitter cries
    like old men clearing their throats

of phlegm; and flapped off
in a wicked silence.

That night the moon was nearing fullness.
There would be light enough
to make Dewato, though return
could be treacherous.

When I set out the wind was strong
from the south, Hoodsport
was a bridge strung with many lights
under Orion,

the waves ploughed the gravel hard.
But leeward of a headland
I found a cove where the moon and the heron
labored as one.

There were freshets then with voices
hooded in smoke, a torn
fawn in a ringmail of maggots
and hooves like obsidian.

I knew that corpse a gentle thing
the moon was careful toward;
bloodworms and small crustaceans
minded the vacant flesh.

But the wind at my back was not kind.
It had the serrate edge
of a flint and struck the water
with a desolate fire.

And when I stood at the rivermouth
in a grove of broken alder,
when I stood beneath the frost trees
that fringe the village there

I felt the draft of an open grave.
The bay was empty,
there was the shack on the gravel spit,
the drained mud, as I

remembered, but the crows were absent,
unless that sudden cloud

had something to do with them
   or the intense cold.

You could have scratched my hands with a stone,
   I'd have felt nothing
but the alder tense to breaking
   and cold binding the soil

with white thongs. The river went still
   as a marble quarry,
shells, piers gleamed on the gravel
   and were gone:

I saw men and women bolt upright
   in the pay of death.
With no more thought than a pool of solder
   at the point of the iron

they were welding metal struts
   to children's collarbones,
fastening the tides of Hood Canal
   with numbered screws and rivets.

I knew this was the Trident then,
   not three but many prongs
to still the heart of the tyee salmon
   and all the living oceans.

They lay in cradles along the piers,
   not a hatch, not a seam was showing
as if the things had spawned themselves
   the final labor of iron.

But there was the dust of Moscow sleeping
   and there St. Petersburg,
the golden dust of the Hermitage
   like wheat in a silo.

I heard the lament from far away,
   a sound of burning pitch,
children trundled in their beds
   over the Baltic.

And all the mothers stood at the doors
   unable to save their darlings,
and all the fathers held in their hands
   were bonnets of flame.

Basalt cracked and rang like bronze.
    The Brothers were shorn where they stood.
A hundred feet tall the wave
    that broke on Annas Bay.

This I saw while Orion was setting
    and the Ploughman stood on the hill—
a rootless tree, an ebbing tide,
    the moon a tilted stone,

the shadow of a man with his arms raised up
    inside a flake of charcoal,
veins of blood, veins of metal
    pounded in a mortar.

Side by side I heard them keening
    as if troubled in their sleep—
gulls in the winter moonlight there,
    the blistered mouthless children.

But quieter than gulls, far off, unseen
    little ones were singing
as if I stood in a churchyard
    and listened to the choir within:

Who is that hurling the bloodstone
    from the middle of the sky?
Why does the ant run round and round
    as if afraid to die?

Why does dust keep blowing and blowing
    and never a thing get born?
How can a gift as dear as the Earth
    ever be returned?

I heard other tongues than our own,
    things, I thought, that could never
weep, as if chalk had mouths
    and stones could speak.

Then across the Canal a dog barked once,
    the voices stilled like crickets
when you stir: Dewato was again
    only moonlight and the river.

I started home and it was strange
    to feel shells underfoot
when I had seen death scour the earth
    of all but dust and wind.

At Keflavik

Rockweed and manwrack—
rotting stolons of kelp, iron pipes, porous
lava stone—the tideland at Keflavik.
Black-backed gulls,
portentous as ravens, veer and scream
over the splintered, squared masonry
of basalt, the subtler mutilations
of sea-devoured metal. Rings and bolts
in the rough-cast concrete
rain away, a lichen-slow
dissolution. Nearby,
the dry-docked rusting hull of a trawler
is like the catafalque
of some immense, gracefully boned sea bird.

Letter to Scardanelli

Here by alder fire,
I write you, Scardanelli,
the ground stone-hard,
whited by frost
and the wheeling stars.
It is late
in another century;
a satellite, perhaps
a warhead, glides
between the arms of Orion.
(Do you understand?
These weapons
of the nation states,
like their hatreds,
are abstract; we have
new words such as
megaton and megadeath.)
Below the house and its park
of Old World trees—
red oak and hornbeam—
the river queries
its bank, asks each
overarching alder,
each embedded shell,
You? You?
and passes on,
intently probing.
What are poets for
in a dark time?
By day, the shrike
hunts by the river
and the kingfisher,
the halcyon, you would say,
eyes the steelheader
who casts from the bridge.
I watch him
take his limit
and drive off toward
dusk. By night,

I read "Patmos" and the Saxon
poets, for the same reason
I study winter
constellations. Because
we do not survive the Earth
a godlike vision
breaks us. As this century,
this charnel house
of sad utopias,
also breaks us.
But the gods, you say,
have withdrawn:
we're all as those herdsmen
in the dry mountains
where cannisters of nerve gas
explode at random.
We hold out
in a time without worth.
Like an amulet
we no longer trust
but cannot abandon,
we call upon language.

By La Push

for Pablo Neruda

It is Wednesday morning and eternity.
For ten thousand miles the Pacific
staggers against the coast, and cormorants
race the troughs of breaking waves.
For ten thousand miles sea mews and kittiwakes,
insomnia of foghorns, gull-scudded headlands,
and nobody gets any sleep.

It sloshes the char and salt of Isla Negra
where a moon-bellied grebe has washed ashore,
it tugs at stolons of kelp, and churns up clouds
of petrels—the same bedlam
today as always, same cries of the oystercatcher,
sad clairvoyant of the tideland.
And nobody gets any sleep here.

Consider the mollusk, he's either clamped down
or dead. Consider the fiddler crab
playing shell games with turban snails.
Christ, it's like a circus
where all the masks have large mouths.
Spiny urchins, Anthopleuras, rhinoceros
auklets: nobody gets any sleep.

Like suffering vertigo in an all-night house
of mirrors, try to claim your body—
that squat thing like a hand sheathed in horn?
That coil of intestine with a jaw
locally known as Aristotle's Lantern? That night-luminous
frilled carrot some fool called a sea pen?
Pronounce your name without slurring?
You can't even walk a straight line.

Go read your Ovid, go read your Darwin—
we're derelicts without identities.
It's always Wednesday in this drunk tank,
and nobody gets any sleep.

Under Snaefellsjokull

Good Friday 1981

1

Now the gannet
falls, bowlike with lancet
beak, and a funnel of kittiwakes
catches the light
turning toward the headland.

Moon-radiant the glacier
hangs over the caldera,
the seared map of lava and ash,
serrate coast
where the cormorant
is a dark crucifix.

Under the cinderpit,
fulmars like iron filings
or a hatch of flies, only white
or mottled gray, swirl and cling
to the seaward cliffs.
Tube-nostrilled, reptilian,
yet blooded like us,
they scavenge the small dead
stiffened in algae
or shroud the gunwales
of open boats.

While the gannet plunges
and the moon-horned glacier
floats over the crescent bay,
the gimleted cliffs of Stapi:
again and again, the stabbing
descent of the stiff-winged bird.

2

You shared the feast,
ate with us fish and fowl,

sweet and sour contagion of flesh
and felt the ache of generation.

Hunger pulled you down.
Through your spine
with its segments of a worm,
ran the chord
toward the changeless
hours of the sea urchin.

You too were coiled
in Adam's genitals,
in the thallus of the first lichen,
fronds of brown algae
bubbled with seed
and the gray caul of childless rock.

Yeast-grapes changing
the wine worked in your veins.
As the woman knelt
by the pool in parched
summer, ringed by lime
and whited knobs of ivy,
you knew pathos
like the salt stains
on the spade's handle.

3

Nailed there,
your tendons pulled tight
as gut on some stringed
instrument, the spear
plucked the cry
from your viscera.
You were all men
dying, a starward breath
stapled to bone,
the ash torn down,
its rootball of blood and clay
blanched in the sun.

And the maggot wept for the flesh it mouthed,
the plankton in the wave bloomed into consciousness,

ants in the furrowed darkness, the worm
cut by the gliding ploughshare,
saw the skulled larvae.
The tern swiveling with a metallic
cry, the diving gannet
braided to the sea beneath,
mourned with the maiden under the Tree.

That moment the planet held
a single grief note
before the mouths
jerked open again.

For us your body
strung harplike on the sad Tree,
your eyes in death
preying on the infinite, gentle predator,
your triumphant plunge from all dust,
is too much.

We are not such victors.

For us, the wyrm cut on the church door,
the insoluble maze on the headland,
for us, the seal sliding in the wave,
the scurrying beetle.

We cannot follow you, swallow
unlocked even from your bones.
The sea bird is veined,
beaked, and conceived in blood,
yet more than these,
man is streaked and mottled,
thigh and jaw deep
in the same bath.

4

The legend was always
wound could lance wound
and the incised cup
lifted with care
wash clear
the blood-shot eye

as the sands at Buthir—
each grain chased
by the wave's violence,
a wreckage of shell
beautiful as cinnabar—
and these wings of white-yellow
winter grass
are the wan gold
of undreamt-of redemption.

Homesick, you will return
through mazes of carbon
and gaze on the cormorant
drying its wings
to dive again in the dark bay,
a gliding mouth, an emblem.

You will return to the salt edge,
the old wound
with its makeshift bandages of kelp,
rotting ledges
where carcasses of sheep
bloat and breathe
in the sea's iron lungs.

It was always beyond healing —
this blood-wreathed, bacterial ooze,
crab-husk and ebb-shine
like flowers of sulfur,
the membrane stench,
rank and inviolable.

They are flesh
forever, Lord —
the spearfall gannet,
the snakebird poised
on the lava spine,
mollusk, sea worm
and we with them.

A History of Rain

So you arrive in the old country of rain.
The road sign says Mist, Jewell,
Vernonia. Woodsmoke
is rising against the rain
so slowly, you wonder if time
is passing, and did the alders
have leaves this year? Walk on
through a covered bridge and the sun
pours through a thousand knotholes
in lasers of smoking light.
When you emerge it is raining
as it only rains in the first chapter of Genesis,
a rain without ambiguity and guile,
a rain with pointed arches and high clerestories
where the aquiline features of saints
are smoothed away like a child's
in sleep. You discover
your vocation: you will write
the history of rain, you will set down
on usnea and moss the lineage of mist,
the martyrdom of clouds. You will record
the resurrections rain accomplishes,
its infinite extension and seeming absence,
as if it fell to no purpose
but to elicit meditation,
the pause of the scribe before the window,
transparence of a mind
given over to rain.

Permissions

Many of these poems first appeared in the following periodicals,
and permission to reprint is gratefully acknowledged:
Mississippi Mud, no. 22, "Late Winter Sky"; *permafrost*, "Letter to Scardanelli"
and "A Road in the Willapa Hills"; *Fine Madness*, "Hanging at Galgahraun" and
"Some Gnomic Verses"; *The Malahat Review* 57, "Afterlight"; *Jawbone* 2,
no. 1 (1976), "For Wang Wei"; *The Montana Review*, no. 2, "A German Print-
maker"; *Poetry Northwest*, "Red Cedar" and "Summer, Aeneas Valley"; *Hiram
Poetry Review*, no. 28, "George Vancouver's Death Dream"; *Willow Springs
Magazine*, "Dewato" and "Under Snaefellsjokull"; *Poetry Seattle*, "Voices
Overheard on a Night of the Perseid Shower"; *Porch*, "Afterlight"; *The Seattle
Review* 1, no. 1 (1978), "Okanogan Sleep"; *Poetry*, "Winter, Aeneas Valley,"
"Home," and "Elegy for Martin Heidegger"; *Shenandoah:* The Washington
and Lee University Review, "Dusting the Sill," copyright 1975 by Washington
and Lee University; *CutBank*, no. 7 (published at the University of Montana),
"Island"; *New England Review, Bread Loaf Quarterly* 3, no. 4, "Reading
Chretien by Hood Canal"; *Sewanee Review* 91 (Summer 1983), "Last Rites" and
"A History of Rain"; *California Quarterly*, "Painter at Dusk," copyright 1977
by the Regents of the University of California; *Prairie Schooner* 49, no. 2 (1975),
"Hawk," copyright © 1975 University of Nebraska Press.
Some of these poems were originally published in the form of a chapbook, *Island*
(Seattle: Jawbone Press, 1977).

THE
JUNIPER
PRIZE

This volume is the ninth recipient
of the Juniper Prize
presented annually by the
University of Massachusetts Press
for a volume of original poetry.
The prize is named in honor of Robert Francis,
who has lived for many years at
Fort Juniper, Amherst, Massachusetts.